Poké Rap

I want to be the very best there ever was
To beat all the rest, yeah, that's my cause

Catch 'em, Catch 'em, Gotta catch 'em all

Pokémon I'll search across the land
Look far and wide
Release from my hand
The power that's inside

Catch 'em, Catch 'em, Gotta catch 'em all
Pokémon!

Gotta catch 'em all, Gotta catch 'em all
Gotta catch 'em all, Gotta catch 'em all

At least one hundred and fifty or more to see
To be a Pokémon Master is my destiny

Catch 'em, Catch 'em, Gotta catch 'em all
Gotta catch 'em all, Pokémon! (repeat three times)

Can you rap all 150?

**Here's the next 32.
Check out book #13
Race to Danger
for more of the Poké Rap.**

Alakazam, Goldeen, Venonat, Machoke
Kangaskhan, Hypno, Electabuzz, Flareon
Blastoise, Poliwhirl, Oddish, Drowzee
Raichu, Nidoqueen, Bellsprout, Starmie

Metapod, Marowak, Kakuna, Clefairy
Dodrio, Seadra, Vileplume, Krabby
Lickitung, Tauros, Weedle, Nidoran
Machop, Shellder, Porygon, Hitmonchan

Words and Music by Tamara Loeffler and John Siegler
Copyright © 1999 Pikachu Music (BMI)
Worldwide rights for Pikachu Music administered by Cherry River Music Co. (BMI)
All Rights Reserved   Used by Permission

There are more books
about Pokémon.

Collect them all!

POKÉMON™

Scyther, Heart of a Champion

Adapted by Sheila Sweeney

Scholastic Ltd
London - New York - Toronto - Sydney - Auckland
Mexico City - New Delhi - Hong Kong

Scholastic Children's Books
Commonwealth House, 1-19 New Oxford Street
London WC1A 1NU
A division of Scholastic Ltd
London - New York - Toronto - Sydney - Auckland
Mexico City - New Delhi - Hong Kong

First published in the USA by Scholastic Inc., New York, 2000.
This edition published in the UK by Scholastic Ltd, 2000.

ISBN 0 439 16945 3

10 9 8 7 6 5 4 3 2 1

Printed by Bath Press, England

POKéMON ™

Scyther: Heart of a Champion

Bug Island

"Look! It's Murcott Island!" Ash Ketchum shouted. He pointed to an island covered in thick woods.

Ash and his lightning mouse, Pikachu, rode on Ash's trusty Lapras, a large, blue Water Pokémon. Ash's friends, Misty and Tracey, also rode Lapras. Misty held Togepi, a tiny baby Pokémon that had hatched from a rare egg.

Ash couldn't wait to get to Murcott Island and the next Pokémon adventure.

"Let's go!" Ash called to his friends. He

pulled his red-and-white cap over his shaggy black hair.

Ash wanted to explore the island right away. When he reached the age of ten, Ash had left home to go on a journey to search for new Pokémon — creatures with amazing powers — and to compete against Gym Leaders to earn badges. To become a Pokémon Master, he needed to capture and train all different kinds of Pokémon. His journey had taken him a long way, all the way to the Orange Islands. He and his friends had seen some amazing things on the islands and he hoped Murcott Island wouldn't be any different.

"Aaaahhhhh!" Misty cried as a large Beedrill buzzed overhead. The combination Bug and Flying Pokémon looked like a big, fierce bee. Misty clutched Togepi tightly. Her orange hair gleamed in the sun.

But Tracey looked excited. "Murcott Island is famous for having tons of Bug Pokémon," he said. "We might discover a new Pokémon." Tracey was a Pokémon trainer and watcher. He was a few years

2

older than Ash, and wore a bandana in his dark hair. Tracey was always searching for new Pokémon to study and draw.

Lapras swam up to the island's shore. Ash and his friends jumped off onto the beach.

"Thanks, Lapras," Ash said as he took out a Poké Ball. Ash recalled Lapras and put the ball back on his belt.

Tracey took out two of his Poké Balls. "Marill!" Tracey called, and a blue Pokémon appeared. Marill looked like a plump blue mouse with big ears. A round ball bobbed on the end of its long tail.

"Venonat!" Tracey shouted. A furry, bug-like Pokémon stood next to Marill. Venonat had two round, red eyes, two flat feet and no arms.

Ash and Tracey were eager to start capturing Pokémon. But Misty looked as though she wanted to get back on Lapras and ride out to sea.

"What's the matter with her?" Tracey asked. He looked over at Misty, who was usually fearless.

"Misty's afraid of Bug Pokémon," Ash explained.

"Oh, I get it," Tracey turned to Misty. "When it comes to *bugs*, Misty's a *chicken!*"

"Who are you calling a chicken?" Misty protested.

"Don't worry, Misty," Tracey comforted. "Marill and Venonat will take care of us."

Ash watched as Venonat and Marill headed straight for the woods.

"Venonat's radar and Marill's keen hearing will help us find new Pokémon," Tracey explained.

Ash nodded. Tracey's Pokémon had proven themselves to be very useful on their adventures.

Venonat and Marill led Ash and the

others to a clearing in the forest. A group of small, green Bug Pokémon crawled in the grass. "Cool! Caterpie," Ash said.

Misty took one look at them and turned away. "Yuck! I hate bugs! I hate bugs! I hate bugs!" she chanted as she dragged Ash and Pikachu away.

Suddenly, they heard a noise in the trees. They stopped. A large Pokémon with two sharp horns on top of its brown body jumped in front of them. It raised its terrible claws in the air. It was a Pinsir, Ash knew. The Caterpie looked cute compared to the Pinsir — even to Misty. Misty grabbed Ash's arm. They ran back to find Tracey.

Ash told Tracey all about the scary Pinsir.

"Pinsir are pretty incredible," Tracey said. "But not that unusual. I'm hoping Marill and Venonat will find something really rare."

Suddenly, Venonat and Marill pointed into the woods.

"There's something in that direction!"

Tracey said excitedly. He ran after his Pokémon. Ash and the others followed.

Soon they came to a clearing in the trees.

Venonat and Marill had found something, all right. A big green Pokémon with razor-edged wings was laying on the ground. It looked very, very sick.

Ash quickly took out his Pokédex, Dexter. The small computer held information about all kinds of Pokémon.

"Scyther, the mantis Pokémon. It uses its sharp wings to capture prey. It can also use its wings to fly. It is seldom seen by humans and almost never captured," Dexter explained.

Ash, Misty, Tracey and Pikachu moved forwards to check out Scyther. Suddenly, it opened its eyes and hissed. The friends quickly jumped back.

"It looks angry," Misty commented.

"Let me check out your injuries, Scyther," Tracey whispered gently. He slowly approached the giant creature.

Scyther jumped up. It looked ready to attack the friends at any moment.

"All right, then," Ash said. He took out a Poké Ball to capture Scyther.

"What are you doing, Ash?" Tracey asked.

"I'm going to catch this Scyther. Then I'll take it to the Pokémon Centre so it can get help," Ash replied. He threw the Poké Ball at Scyther. "Go, Poké Ball!" Ash shouted.

The Poké Ball flew through the air. Scyther raised a giant wing. It easily batted the Poké Ball away.

Ash couldn't believe it. Scyther refused to be caught!

"How can Scyther do that?" Misty asked. "It looks so weak."

Ash frowned. Scyther did look weak. Ash knew that he had to get it to the Pokémon Centre soon. But Scyther didn't look as though it would back down easily. In fact, it looked ready for a fight!

Scyther Attack

"If that Scyther wants a fight, it'll get one!" Ash shouted. "Go, Pikachu!"

Pikachu was the very first Pokémon Ash ever had. The small Electric Pokémon always fought bravely for Ash. Even though Scyther was much bigger, Pikachu was ready for the challenge.

"Wait!" Tracey called before Pikachu could get to Scyther. "It's too weak to fight."

"You want me to just leave it here?" Ash asked. "It's a rare Pokémon, Tracey. And it needs help."

"Leave it to me," Tracey replied. "You're up, Venonat," he told his Pokémon.

Venonat carefully approached Scyther. Venonat was not much bigger than Pikachu. It didn't look like a good match for Scyther, either. But Tracey knew Venonat had many powerful poisonous techniques.

"You can do it, Venonat!" he shouted. "Sleep Powder!"

Venonat released the Sleep Powder. The weakened Scyther couldn't resist. It drifted softly into a deep sleep.

"It's working!" Ash exclaimed.

Tracey hurled a Poké Ball at Scyther. The ball opened. Light flashed and the Scyther disappeared.

It was finally caught!

"Quick," Tracey ordered his friends. "Let's get it to a Pokémon Centre!"

As the friends travelled through the forest, they were too busy to notice the giant hot-air balloon flying overhead. Inside the balloon were Jessie, James and Meowth, a trio of Pokémon thieves known as Team Rocket. The balloon looked just like Meowth, a white scratch cat Pokémon.

Team Rocket searched the forest through their binoculars until they spotted Ash and his friends.

"Just the Pokémon trainers we love to steal from," sneered Jessie, a tall teenage girl who wore a white uniform.

"Let's get them!" shouted her partner, James. James had blue hair and wore a uniform just like Jessie's.

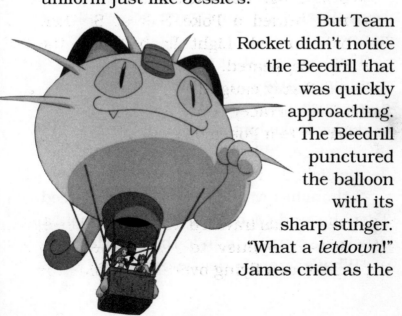

But Team Rocket didn't notice the Beedrill that was quickly approaching. The Beedrill punctured the balloon with its sharp stinger. "What a *letdown*!" James cried as the balloon deflated and sailed back down to land.

Jessie, James and Meowth looked around at all the strange, buglike Pokémon that inhabited Murcott Island.

"Where are we?" Jessie wondered.

"It's certainly *buggy*," James shrugged.

"You can say that again," Meowth said. "There's a swarm of Scyther headed our way!"

Slash! The sound of Scyther's swordlike wings whipped through the air.

Swish! Scyther moved so fast that Team Rocket couldn't even see what was happening.

Team Rocket shut their eyes as a blur of metallic wings surrounded them. They didn't open them until it was quiet again.

Jessie looked up and down. She was still in one piece. "*Whew!* That was a close one!" Jessie sighed with relief.

"I thought I was a goner!" James agreed. Then he and Meowth got a good look at Jessie. They tried to hide their giggles.

"What's wrong?" Jessie demanded.

12

"Um . . . Jessie . . . I'm afraid . . ." James didn't want to tell her the bad news.

". . . your hair's not there!" Meowth purred.

Jessie felt around the top of her head. Where once there was long, flowing, red hair, now there were short chunks. The Scyther had cut off all her hair!

"I'm going to get that Scyther!" Jessie screamed. "Someone is going to pay!"

"Why catch just *one* Scyther when we can swipe the whole *swarm*!?" Meowth asked.

"You think we could do that?" Jessie and James wondered.

"Of course! If we had a swarm of Scyther on our side, we'd be simply unstoppable!" Meowth explained.

"Yes!" James understood. "We can get revenge for Jessie's hair and score points with the boss at the same time!"

"What are we waiting for?" Jessie asked. "I want revenge on those butchering bugs!"

3

Scyther Recovers

"Why did the Scyther keep trying to fight when it was so weak?" Ash wondered.

Ash, Misty and Tracey were at the Pokémon Centre on Murcott Island. Nurse Joy, a red-haired Pokémon expert, worked to heal the injured Scyther. Two round, pink Chansey helped Nurse Joy. The friends waited anxiously outside the operating room.

"Hey, you two," Misty looked through the glass window of the operating room. "Scyther keeps staring at us."

Nurse Joy came out to talk to the friends. "How is Scyther?" Ash asked.

"It's in pretty bad shape," Nurse Joy said regretfully. "It will take quite a while for it to recover."

"What do you think happened to it?" Ash asked. Maybe if they knew the cause of Scyther's injuries, they could help it recover.

Nurse Joy explained, "I guess the old warrior finally lost a battle for leadership of its swarm."

"How do you know that Scyther was the leader of its whole swarm?" Tracey asked.

"Well," Nurse Joy continued, "an older Scyther could only have got *these* kinds of injuries by battling another Scyther."

Ash was still confused. "But if it's so strong, how could it have been defeated?"

"Usually it's a younger, faster Scyther that challenges the leader. Sometimes speed and power can overcome even the most experienced Pokémon," Nurse Joy explained. "Once a leader loses to another Scyther, it can't stay in the swarm. Unless it wins another leadership battle, it has to live all by itself."

Ash was listening closely to Nurse Joy when he heard a ring. "It's the videophone," Ash told Nurse Joy.

Nurse Joy switched on the videophone. Professor Oak, the ultimate authority on Pokémon, appeared on the screen.

Ash had first come to the Orange Islands to pick up the mysterious gold-and-silver GS Ball for Professor Oak.

"Professor Oak," Ash greeted his mentor. "This is my friend, Tracey. He's an excellent Pokémon watcher. He captured the Scyther that Nurse Joy is taking care of."

"You should be very proud of your capture, Tracey," Professor Oak replied. "Congratulations."

Tracey looked embarrassed. "I suppose so."

"Aren't you

happy to have caught it?" Professor Oak asked.

Tracey looked at the Scyther, who was laying in bed. It was still hissing and staring at them. "It doesn't seem to like me," Tracey said sadly.

"Scyther are born with a warrior's pride," Professor Oak told Tracey. "The Scyther must feel it has lost pride by losing first the leadership battle and then being caught by you."

"What can I do to help it?" Tracey asked eagerly.

Professor Oak continued, "Keep in mind that every single Pokémon has its own unique feelings and personality. You must try to help Scyther regain confidence in itself and in its strength."

Ash could see the determination on Tracey's face. He knew Tracey was thinking about Professor Oak's words. Ash watched Tracey go to Scyther's bedside. As Ash stood in the doorway, he could hear Tracey whisper, "I'm sorry, Scyther. You must feel terrible after being captured without a real battle."

Scyther looked at Tracey and hissed weakly.

"But as a trainer, I couldn't just leave you there," Tracey explained. "I never thought I would end up hurting you."

Ash entered the room. "I have an idea, Tracey," he said to his friend. "What if this Scyther has a rematch with the one it lost to? Scyther's a natural born warrior. And it's happiest when it's battling."

As Scyther listened to Ash's words, it turned towards him. It looked a little stronger already.

Tracey turned to Scyther. "What do you think, Scyther? When you're better you can go and battle again! Maybe I can even help you to train if you want me to!"

Suddenly, Scyther began to flap its wings. It floated up above the bed. Nurse Joy and the friends looked alarmed.

"No, wait!" Nurse Joy pleaded. "You can't move yet!"

Scyther flew away from Tracey and

crashed out through the window. The friends called after it. "Scyther! Scyther! Come back! You're not well enough yet!" But it was too late. Scyther flew out of sight.

Ash headed out of the door after Scyther. "Come on," he called to his friends. "I bet Scyther's going to challenge the new leader to a rematch!"

ReVenge Is Not So Sweet

"Hold on," Ash whispered to the others. "Look up ahead."

Ash had spotted Team Rocket hiding in the bushes. They were spying on the swarm of Scyther that had attacked them and cut off Jessie's hair. "It's time for revenge!" Jessie cried.

Jessie pointed a device that looked like a telescope at the swarm. "Now it's payback time!" she shouted. A missile shot out of the end of the device. It flew into the air. Then it exploded, sending yellow, gooey taffy all over the Scyther swarm. All the Scyther were caught in the gummy mess.

As they twisted and turned, trying to escape, Team Rocket blasted another device. This time, a net surrounded the sticky swarm.

"So you thought you could get away with cutting my hair, did you?" Jessie taunted. "Well, now I've cut you *all* down to size!"

The Scyther struggled to slash the net, but they couldn't move. They were too sticky from the taffy missile.

"No!" Ash cried. "Somebody's got to save them!"

At his words, something swooped down from a nearby tree.

Tracey's Scyther! Its *body* may have been weak, but its *heart* was super strong.

Scyther slashed at the top of the net with its sharp wings. The net opened up, and the captured Scyther climbed out.

They were free!

"What's going on?" Jessie asked.

Ash ran out of his hiding place. His friends followed. That's when they noticed

Jessie's chopped-up hair. Ash couldn't help giggling.

"What are *you* looking at?" Jessie challenged them.

"Hey, where did you get that new haircut?" Misty laughed.

"You insult my hair?" Jessie warned. "Prepare for trouble."

Jessie and James shouted a new, improved battle cry:

"To protect the world from pattern baldness.

To fight split ends within our nation.

To denounce bad hair and poor complexion.

To draw jealous stares in our direction.

Jessie!

James!

Team Rocket blast off with haloes alight.

Surrender now or prepare to fight."

"*Meowth!* That's right!" added Meowth. "Let's catch Pikachu and all those Scyther at once."

Ash was prepared to battle. "Go Pikachu!" Ash commanded.

"*Pika,*" Pikachu squeaked as it lunged at Team Rocket. James quickly took out a Poké Ball. He released a Pokémon that looked like a purple cloud of smog with two heads. It was Weezing, a combination Poison and Gas Pokémon.

"Weezing, Smokescreen!" James ordered.

A gray fog covered Ash and his friends.

They began to cough and choke. Pikachu was helpless. *Oh, no,* Ash thought. *We might actually lose to Team Rocket!*

Then there was a whir in the air. Ash looked up. Tracey's Scyther was spinning like a top, creating a strong wind. The wind cleared away all the smog!

"What's that?" Ash asked Dexter as he began to breathe more easily.

"Swords Dance, Scyther's special attack. Scyther spins furiously to focus its energy and increase its attack power," Dexter explained.

Scyther folded its wings. It landed on the ground in front of Meowth. *"Scy, scy,"* it warned in a raspy voice.

Meowth understood most Pokémon language. The catlike Pokémon nodded. "Yeah, yeah, you talk pretty big."

"What did it say?" James asked Meowth.

Meowth spoke in its deepest voice. "It's

saying, 'I may not be their leader any more, but I won't let you take them.'"

But Team Rocket wasn't going to give up so easily.

"Arbok!" Jessie shouted as she threw a Poké Ball in the air. A Poison Pokémon that looked like a cobra appeared.

"Victreebel!" called James. He released a Pokémon that looked like a giant yellow plant.

Jessie threw one more ball in the air. "Lickitung!" she yelled. A pink-and-white Pokémon with a long, sticky tongue burst from the Poké Ball.

"Weezing, Victreebel!" James commanded. "Tear it apart!"

"You, too, Arbok and Lickitung!" Jessie added.

Team Rocket's Pokémon advanced on Tracey's Scyther. Pikachu ran in to help.

But Scyther lifted a wing and held Pikachu back. It didn't want any help. It needed to fight this battle all by itself.

"It's battling to win back its pride as a warrior!" Tracey exclaimed.

Scyther looked back at Tracey. It knew that Tracey now understood. It was ready to obey Tracey's commands.

Meowth challenged Scyther first.

"Attack!" Tracey shouted. Scyther let out a great roar. It raised a great wing and slashed Meowth. Meowth tumbled through the air.

"Well done, Scyther," Tracey called.

Scyther hovered in the air, waiting for the next attack. Ash saw Lickitung and Victreebel sneaking up beneath the warrior Pokémon. Tracey noticed it, too. Lickitung was coming from the left. Victreebel was coming from the right.

"Look out below, Scyther!" Tracey shouted.

Scyther flew up just in the nick of time. Instead of grabbing Scyther, Lickitung and Victreebel crashed into each other.

The battle
wasn't over.
Arbok slithered
up into the air.
Ash knew that
Scyther needed to
watch out for its
poison sting.
"Quick Attack,"
commanded
Tracey.

Scyther danced from side to side around Arbok. Arbok tried to attack Scyther. But Scyther was too fast. Arbok missed and fell to the ground.

Victreebel recovered and returned to battle. But Scyther quickly used the Slash Attack to cut off a few of Victreebel's leaves and the Pokémon retreated.

"It worked!" Ash cried, but he was still worried. Scyther was weak and out of breath. He wasn't sure how much more fighting it could take before it fainted.

"Arbok, Poison Needle!" Jessie commanded.

The snakelike Pokémon shot out sharp, poison-drenched spikes that rained down on Scyther. Scyther was too weak to retaliate.

Ash cringed. "Don't let them win, Scyther!" he called out. But in his heart, he knew that Scyther was too weak to win this battle after all.

5

An old Friend to the Rescue

Scyther writhed in pain. Arbok closed in to finish the attack. It shot a new barrage of poison needles at Scyther.

Ash turned away. He couldn't bear to look.

But the sound of wings made him turn back. A blurry figure flew in front of Scyther. It was the new leader of the Scyther swarm! The young Scyther deflected the needles with its wings.

"It defended our Scyther!" Tracey shouted happily.

Jessie looked determined. "Then all of you attack at once," she ordered her Pokémon.

Team Rocket's Pokémon were now as weak as Scyther once was. Tracey and Scyther worked together to defeat them easily. Scyther raised its shiny wings to fight off another attack from Arbok. Then Scyther crossed its wings, one over the other. Energy flashed from the razor-tips and slammed into Team Rocket's Pokémon. The blast knocked them all down.

Jessie had one last hope. She raised the taffy missile device and screamed, "I've still got one more shot!"

"Pikachu!" Ash ordered. "Thunderbolt."

Pikachu sent out a fierce bolt that electrified Jessie, James, and Meowth. They ran as fast as they could into the trees. But before they could get away, Scyther used one last Slash Attack to chop off their hair. All that was left was one stripe down the middle of each of their heads.

Ash, Misty and Tracey laughed at Team Rocket's new look. A swarm of Beedrill flew

overhead. A parade of Caterpie crawled up a nearby tree.

"Um," Misty began tentatively. "Do you think we could get off this bug-infested island now?"

Ash and Tracey smiled. "Okay, Misty." Ash and the others made their way to shore, with Scyther and its swarm flying right behind them.

As Ash released Lapras, Tracey watched as Scyther said good-bye to its old swarm before returning to its Poké Ball. Then the friends climbed on Lapras's back and set out to sea.

It wasn't long before they spotted another island. Luscious green trees full of tropical fruit filled its shores. "Let's stop here," Ash suggested as his stomach growled loudly. "I'm hungry!"

"This looks like a good place," Misty agreed. "I could use a good, bug-free rest!"

"Lapras, take us to that island," Ash instructed.

The friends soon reached the island's shore. Pikachu couldn't wait to start exploring. *"Pika, pika,"* it called to Togepi.

"Togi, togi!" gurgled the baby Pokémon.

"Don't go too far away, you two," Ash warned as they ran off to play.

Ash, Misty and Tracey explored the shore, looking for some lunch. Just then, a nut fell from the sky. It hit Ash right on the head. Ash

looked up. He saw a strange tan Pokémon flying overhead. "Hey that looks like . . ." Ash began.

Dexter finished his sentence. "Farfetch'd, the wild duck Pokémon. This extremely rare Pokémon can always be found holding a leek or green onion, which it uses to build its nest."

Tracey was excited by this discovery. "This is very unusual!" he said. "I need to observe this."

"Let's observe lunch first," Misty suggested.

"There are so many fruits and berries on this island that finding food shouldn't be a problem," Tracey replied as he picked some tropical fruit off a tree.

"Great! Let's rest here all day," Ash suggested. "Our Pokémon could use a break."

Ash threw four Poké Balls into the air. "Squirtle, Bulbasaur, Charizard, Snorlax, come on out!" Ash called as he released his Pokémon. Squirtle looked like a cute turtle.

Bulbasaur had a plant bulb growing on its back. Charizard was a combination Fire and Flying Pokémon that looked like an orange dragon. And the sleepy Snorlax was one of the biggest and laziest Pokémon around.

Misty specialized in Water Pokémon. She released Staryu, a star-shaped Pokémon, and Goldeen, an elegant Pokémon that looked like a beautiful goldfish, and sent them to play in the waves with Lapras.

Finally, Tracey took out two Poké Balls. "Venonat! Marill!"

The Pokémon all played happily on the beach. Marill let Topegi use its round tail like a toy. Then Ash noticed that Tracey had forgotten to release his newest

combination Bug and Flying Pokémon, Scyther.

Tracey threw the Poké Ball into the air. Scyther appeared at last. It growled and hissed. The other Pokémon gasped and jumped back. They eyed its sharp, sparkling wings.

"Oh," Ash chuckled. "None of you have met Scyther yet, have you? Everyone, say hello to Scyther!"

The Pokémon greeted Scyther timidly. Scyther replied with a bellowing roar.

"You're supposed to say hello, not scare them half to death!" Misty informed Scyther. She picked Togepi up and held it tightly in her arms.

Togepi wiggled its way out of Misty's arms. It hopped down and over to Scyther. "*Togi, togi*," it squeaked.

Scyther looked down at the adorable baby Pokémon and stopped growling. When the other Pokémon saw that Togepi was okay, they walked over to Scyther, one by one.

All but Charizard, that is. Ever since Ash

had evolved Charizard from Charmeleon, he'd had trouble getting the Pokémon to obey his commands.

"Introduce yourself to Scyther, too, Charizard," Ash suggested.

Charizard turned away from Ash. "Come on, Charizard! Listen to me!" Ash whined.

Charizard turned and breathed a ball of fire aimed right at Ash. But the fireball shot past Ash. It hit Scyther by mistake!

Scyther flew in front of Charizard's face and roared loudly.

"Charizard, no!" Ash yelled.

"Scyther, back down!" Tracey commanded.

But the two Pokémon didn't budge. They eyed each other angrily.

"I think they're going to fight!" Ash cried.

6

A Day to Rest?

Ash bravely stepped in between Scyther and Charizard. "No fighting! This is supposed to be a day off!" he shouted.

Scyther and Charizard backed off. They continued to growl at each other. They had definitely *not* got off to a good start.

"This looks like a pretty hopeless situation," Misty observed. "I don't think they'll ever get along!"

"Maybe they'll be in a better mood after they eat," Tracey suggested. "It's time we found lunch!"

Ash and his friends spent the morning wandering around the island. They searched for food, and found lots of fruits and vegetables. They set up a camp on the shore. Then they started to cook.

Snorlax plodded over and gobbled down all of their food in one bite.

"Snorlax, no!" Ash cried. His stomach growled as he looked at the now empty cooking pot. Not even a crumb was left. "Our dinner gone in one bite," he said.

With a full stomach, Snorlax lay back and instantly fell asleep.

"Snorlax certainly isn't shy about eating when it wants to eat and sleeping when it wants to sleep, is it?" Tracey commented.

"Maybe not," Misty said as she pulled some extra fruit and vegetables out of her bag, "but at least Snorlax didn't find these." The three friends smiled.

"Lunch is ready!" Ash called. All the Pokémon stopped splashing in the water and swinging in the trees. They ran over to the camp for some food. This time, there was one more Pokémon tagging along.

"What is Jigglypuff doing here?" Misty asked as she noticed the pink, big-eyed Pokémon.

"Oh no!" Ash cried. Ash knew that Jigglypuff loved to sing. Ash also knew that Jigglypuff's Sing Attack would send them all into dreamland.

"Let's get out of here," Tracey added.

But nobody had a chance to go anywhere. Jigglypuff began to sing its mesmerizing lullaby. Ash, Misty, Tracey and all the Pokémon were soon fast asleep.

When they awoke, Jigglypuff was gone. But it left a memento. Everyone had squiggles and swirls on their faces. Jigglypuff had written all over them with its black marker!

Ash shook his head. It happened every time. Jigglypuff got angry when its audience fell asleep. The marker was its revenge.

Ash and his friends were hungrier than ever. They washed off all the marker. Then they let Snorlax sleep a little longer while they quickly ate up the fruit and vegetables from Misty's bag. Scyther and Charizard growled at each other as they ate.

"I guess the food isn't solving their problem," Misty observed.

As Ash tried to keep Scyther and Charizard far apart, another problem was creeping up on a ledge behind the camp: Team Rocket.

"What a coincidence!" Jessie remarked. "We came here to relax and we found the twerps instead!"

"*Meowth!*" purred Meowth.

"No problem," James said. "Who needs

rest when we can finally capture Pikachu?"

James threw a Poké Ball in the air. Victreebel popped out.

"Sleep Powder!" James commanded.

Victreebel's Sleep Powder drifted over the camp. In seconds, Ash and everyone else at the camp was asleep once again.

"Victreebel's Sleep Powder almost works too well," remarked Meowth.

"That's because I've trained it so well," answered James. "Well done, Victreebel." James tried to compliment his Pokémon,

but Victreebel sucked him up into its giant bell flower mouth.

"I'm your trainer, not your lunch!" James protested.

Jessie pulled James free.

"Come on, master trainer," Jessie sneered. "We've got Pokémon to capture."

Team Rocket fired long ropes down to the camp. Each rope had a suction cup on the end. The ropes flew through the air, and a suction cup attached to each Pokémon. Jessie and James reeled the Pokémon in.

"This is going to be so easy!" James sniggered. "We'll have all the Pokémon before Ash even knows what hit him!"

7

Back to Battle

As Jessie and James struggled to pull in the Pokémon, Scyther and Charizard woke up. Scyther used its slashing wings to cut the ropes and free the other Pokémon. The group of Pokémon ran back to camp and huddled around their trainers.

Ash heard the roars of Charizard and Scyther and bolted up out of his sleep.

"What's happening?" Misty asked sleepily as she opened her eyes.

"I'm not sure," Tracey answered, still half asleep, too.

Team Rocket ran into the camp. "We didn't mean to wake 'em all," Meowth told Ash, "but now we're going to take 'em all!"

"Prepare yourselves!" Jessie and James warned.

"We'll never give up our Pokémon!" Ash said fiercely as he gathered the Pokémon close to him.

"We could beat *you* three in our sleep!" Misty added.

Team Rocket released Arbok and Weezing on the camp. Weezing's choking smog soon filled the air. But this time the friends weren't worried. They knew Scyther's Swords Dance would clear the air in no time. And they were right! Once again, the mantis Pokémon began to spin in place. The spinning made a swirl of air that looked like a mini-tornado. Soon all the smog was whisked away.

Ash looked at Scyther with concern. It was still weak, and the Swords Dance had drained its energy. It was going to need some help.

"Bulbasaur!" Ash commanded. "Vine Whip!"

The plant bulb on Bulbasaur's back opened up. Long green vines snapped through the air and hit Arbok. They stung the Poison Pokémon.

"Perfect!" Ash exclaimed. "Squirtle, Water Gun!"

Squirtle sprayed Jessie, James, and Meowth with a stream of water. The blast sent them flying through the air.

"Now, Pikachu!" Ash called. "Thunder-shock!"

A jolt that looked like lightning shot across the air and electrified Team Rocket.

When Charizard saw the battle, it wanted to join in too. The large Pokémon exhaled a trail of fire right at Team Rocket.

"Ouch!" Team Rocket yelled. "Hot! Hot! Hot!" Tracey looked at Scyther. He knew it would help its pride if Scyther could win the battle. "Scyther! Finish it with Skull Bash!"

A bright flash of energy surrounded Scyther and then Scyther smashed into Team Rocket. Team Rocket blasted off as fast as they had appeared.

"Well done, everyone!" Ash cheered.

The Pokémon all looked around proudly. All except for Scyther and Charizard.

The two large Pokémon were growling at each other. It looked as though another battle might break out at any moment!

8

A Near Miss

"*Char!*" roared the lizard Pokémon.

"*Scy!*" hissed the mantis Pokémon.

Ash looked concerned. Scyther and Charizard had so much in common. They were both powerful Pokémon. But there were definitely bad feelings between them. Would these two *ever* learn to be friends?

"Break it up, you two!" Ash told them.

"Ash, I don't think they want to fight," Misty suggested. "I think they're just acting tough."

"I think she's right," Tracey agreed.

"They've seen that they can use their great powers together to win a battle."

"I hope you're right," Ash said. "That would be one less worry."

Ash threw a Poké Ball in the air. "Charizard, return!" he called. Ash, Tracey, and Misty recalled their Pokémon and headed down to the beach where Lapras, their living water taxi, waited happily. They hopped on Lapras and sailed out on the crisp blue waves of the sea.

"Well, we got a little rest on that island," Ash chuckled.

"But I didn't think we'd need Jigglypuff and Victreebel's Sleep Powder to get it," Misty added.

"*Pika, pika!*" Pikachu remarked. The friends all laughed as they sailed along in the blue-green water.

It was an amazing day. A few puffy white clouds dotted the clear blue sky. A soft breeze cooled the friends. Soothing waves gently rocked them. They leaned back on Lapras. The friends were enjoying the peaceful ride, until . . .

Crash! Splash!
Something was heading
right for Lapras!

"Look out!" Tracey
shouted. A giant wave
nearly knocked the
friends into the sea.
Tracey, Ash, and
Misty had to
hold onto

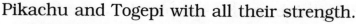

Pikachu and Togepi with all their strength.

"We're going to crash!" Misty yelled as
she spotted a boat headed their way. The
boat's power and speed were causing waves
to swell in the sea. It seemed there was no
way to avoid disaster.

At the last second, the boat swerved
around Lapras. It missed hitting them by
inches. "Hey, watch where you're going!"
came a voice from the boat.

Misty was furious. "Watch where *we're*
going? That was totally reckless! You could
have hurt somebody! *You* should apologize!"

Ash looked up to see a boy taller than
Tracey. He had dark hair. "I'm sorry," the

boy said. "My name's Mugsy." Mugsy smiled and added, "You must be Ash."

Ash blushed. "I am. How did you know?"

"I heard at the gym that you're a pretty powerful trainer," Mugsy explained.

"I guess," Ash said casually. But he was pleased with the remark. While sailing the Orange Islands, he had been battling to earn badges so he could compete in the Orange League. So far he had done pretty well.

Misty burst his bubble. "He doesn't know how to fight with anything but power," she teased.

"That's okay," Mugsy laughed. "I really like strong Pokémon and strong trainers. What do you say, Ash? Would you test your strength against mine?"

Ash looked around. He was honoured by the compliments, but a little embarrassed in front of his friends. Still, he had never turned down a battle yet.

"I accept!" Ash answered.

"Hop on board," Mugsy offered. Misty, Tracey, Ash, and Pikachu climbed on Mugsy's boat. Ash recalled Lapras.

"See that," Mugsy said as he pointed to a tiny speck in the sea ahead of them. "We'll have the battle on that deserted island over there."

Mugsy's speedboat got them to the island in no time. As they stood on the shore, Mugsy challenged, "How about a two against two battle?"

"You're on!" Ash confidently accepted the challenge. He whispered to Pikachu. "I'm counting on you, Pikachu. Let's win this first one." Ash knew his Electric friend would never let him down.

"I see," Mugsy countered. "An Electric Type. Okay, then I'll use this guy!"

Mugsy released Poliwrath, a purple Water and Fighting Pokémon with a black swirl in the middle of its stomach. Ash and Pikachu had never seen this kind of Pokémon before. They looked confused. Ash pulled out Dexter.

"Poliwrath, the tadpole Pokémon," Dexter said. "It is an outstanding swimmer. Poliwrath has well-developed muscles. This makes its fighting attacks formidable."

"*Pika, pika,*" Pikachu squeaked as it

pointed to the belt around Poliwrath's waist.

"What's that belt?" Misty asked.

"That's the belt Poliwrath won in the championship back in my hometown," Mugsy said. "I told you, Ash. I like powerful Pokémon. That belt proved Poliwrath's strength."

"But Water Pokémon are weak against Electric Pokémon," Misty whispered to Ash. "Pikachu should win this battle easily."

Mugsy and Poliwrath heard Misty. They looked at each other and laughed.

Mugsy's confidence made Ash a little
nervous. But he didn't
show it. Ash and
Pikachu bravely
faced Mugsy
and Poliwrath.
"Be careful, Ash!"
Tracey warned.
"There must be a
reason he's using
a Water Pokémon."

9

Power Play

"Go, Pikachu!" Ash commanded. "Thunderbolt!"

Pikachu crackled with electricity. The cute, yellow Pokémon released a stunning bolt. Poliwrath was hit with a blinding flash. Most Pokémon would have been knocked down by the attack. But Poliwrath wasn't even weakened.

"Poliwrath!" Mugsy ordered. "Double Team!"

Ash watched in amazement as the muscular Poliwrath quickly multiplied. Now

there were two Poliwrath instead of one! The team circled around Pikachu.

"Pikachu!" Ash warned. "Don't get taken in. Quick Attack!"

Faster than the blink of an eye, Pikachu released another mighty jolt of electricity. The shock hit the team of Poliwrath and forced them to merge back into one. The Double Team was over. But Poliwrath still looked strong.

"Hypnosis!" Mugsy called to Poliwrath.

Poliwrath turned and faced Pikachu. It looked directly into Pikachu's eyes. Pikachu was dazed. Poliwrath had put Pikachu into a trance!

"Now, Poliwrath," Mugsy shouted. "Water Gun!"

A stream of water burst from Poliwrath like a fire hose. Pikachu was sent flying through the air. When Pikachu landed, Ash could see that it had fainted. Pikachu had lost the battle!

"What happened?" Ash asked his friends. He was so sure he and Pikachu would win this battle.

"It's psychology," Tracey explained. "Mugsy used Poliwrath because he knew you would think Pikachu could easily beat it. He got you to lower your guard."

"Both a trainer and his Pokémon have to be pretty experienced to do something like that," Misty added.

"Who wants to see a fight won by type alone?" Mugsy explained. "A great trainer shows his training skill in battle."

"I know just the warrior to battle your Poliwrath," Tracey said as he unleashed Scyther.

"No, Tracey," Ash said. "This is my battle."

Ash wasn't going to lose to Mugsy so quickly. If Mugsy liked power, well then, he'd get some power. Ash grabbed a Poké Ball and threw it into the air.

Tracey recalled Scyther. He hoped his friend wouldn't act foolishly.

"He couldn't mean . . ." Misty wondered.

"Go, Charizard!" Ash commanded.

Tracey and Misty cringed with fear. They knew how much trouble Ash had get-

ting Charizard
to obey his
commands.
Would the
stubborn
Pokémon
listen to
him now?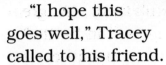

"I hope this
goes well," Tracey
called to his friend.

"Don't worry," Ash replied. "I know Charizard can do this for me."

On hearing its name, Charizard turned and looked at Ash. Then it opened its monstrous mouth. A blast of fire shot right past Ash's face.

"It won't even listen to its trainer?" Mugsy chuckled. "Why would you even take out a Pokémon like that?"

"You're wrong," Ash said. "Show him, Charizard!"

As usual, Charizard wouldn't listen to Ash's commands. It flew up in the air. It soared down and grazed the top of the water.

"Charizard!" Ash shouted. "Charizard! Come on! Get revenge for Pikachu!"

But the powerful Pokémon would not obey Ash. In fact, it flew right by Ash and knocked him down with its tremendous tail.

"Come on, Charizard," Ash pleaded. "We're friends, right? Show him!"

Charizard turned to Ash. Once again it spat blazing fire in Ash's direction.

"Ouch!" Ash yelled.

"It's not listening to Ash," said Tracey. Tracey's Scyther roared in agreement.

Scyther knew that it could do a better job fighting this battle.

"This isn't the first time," added Misty. "But it seems worse than usual."

"This is hopeless," Mugsy sniggered. "I'll show you how a real Pokémon battle should be fought. Poliwrath, Water Gun!"

Once more, Poliwrath unleashed a stream of water. That made Charizard angry. It roared a ball of flame at Poliwrath. But the skilled Pokémon quickly jumped out of the way.

"That Poliwrath is pretty high level," Misty noticed with admiration.

"Settle down, Charizard," Ash said to his Pokémon. "Use something other than fire to attack. Megapunch!"

Charizard heard the command. But it ignored Ash. Instead, it tried to use its powerful flame to singe the Water Pokémon. Poliwrath quickly countered with a fountain of water.

"That's no good, Charizard," Ash tried to explain. "Fire won't work against this Poliwrath."

"This is getting boring," Mugsy yawned. "I think it's about time to tie things up. Poliwrath, Cold Beam!"

A chill froze the air. Poliwrath held its palms together. It created a glowing white ball of ice in between its hands. Poliwrath threw the ball at Charizard. Ash tried to warn his Pokémon. But Charizard wouldn't listen.

The Cold Beam hit Charizard and trapped the Fire Pokémon in a block of ice. The powerful lizard Pokémon was now powerless.

"Charizard! Are you okay? Ash asked.

"Well done, Poliwrath," said Mugsy as he patted his prize Pokémon. Mugsy returned Poliwrath to its Poké Ball. "How about a rematch when you learn to handle that thing?" he called to Ash as he walked down the beach.

Misty, Tracey, and Ash gathered around the frozen Charizard.

"This is really serious, Ash," Tracey quietly told his friend. "I'm not sure Charizard will fully recover."

10

Things Get Hot

"Charizard *will* recover," Ash said with determination. "I may not be able to train it, but I will do everything I can to heal Charizard."

"What can we do to help?" Misty asked.

"*Pikachu*," added Pikachu.

"*Togi*," said Misty's baby Pokémon. Even Scyther looked like it wanted to help.

Ash needed a plan.

"We should probably build some fires," Misty suggested. Ash and Tracey agreed. The heat from the fires would melt the ice and warm up Charizard.

Ash, Misty, and Tracey searched the shore for driftwood. Then they built small fires around Charizard.

Ash stayed with Charizard while Tracey and Misty went in search of more wood. The ice dripped slowly from the enormous creature. Ash rubbed away at what remained. His hands were red and sore.

Soon the fires had melted all the ice. But Charizard was still cold to the touch.

"Hang in there, Charizard!" Ash said with concern.

"I found some blankets," Tracey said as he handed them to Ash.

"Look at your hands, Ash," Misty added. "You should massage Charizard through the blankets so you don't hurt them more."

Ash looked down at his chapped hands. "This is nothing compared to the damage Charizard took," he said sadly. He knew it was his fault that Charizard was in such bad shape.

Misty and Tracey covered Charizard with the blankets.

"I think we should rub Charizard, too," Misty suggested to Tracey. Ash, Misty, and Tracey worked into the night. They rubbed Charizard from snout to tail. Pikachu and Togepi helped, too. Even Scyther fanned the fires with its wings. But as much as they tried, it didn't look as though Charizard was getting any better.

Tracey and Misty yawned. "You should get some sleep," Ash told them.

Ash's friends didn't want to leave him.

But they were too tired to argue. Pikachu, Togepi, and Scyther fell asleep soon after. Ash was left alone with the Pokémon that had caused him so much trouble.

"Come on, Charizard," Ash whispered. "Hurry up and get better." As if it were obeying Ash's commands, Charizard opened its eyes. Ash could see a small weak flame inside Charizard's eyes. "That's it, Charizard," said Ash.

Charizard was too weak to keep its eyes open. Ash thought back to all the moments he had shared with the Pokémon. He remembered how cute the lizard was when it was just a little Charmander. He remembered how he'd had to nurse Charmander back to health after it had been abandoned in the rain by a former trainer. He remembered when it had evolved into Charmeleon and when Charmeleon had finally evolved into Charizard.

"Look Charizard," Ash said. "I know I may not be the greatest trainer. And I know you don't want to battle low-level Pokémon. You probably don't listen to me because I am a low-level trainer. But someday, I'll be experienced enough to battle by your side. That's my dream, to battle as a team. And Charizard, I know we'll win."

Charizard tried to get up. It opened its mouth. A puff of smoke blew out, along with a weak roar. Ash knew Charizard was on the way to regaining its fire power. He quickly gathered more wood to build up the fires around Charizard.

"Rest a little more," Ash said sleepily. "You'll be all better in the morning."

When the sun rose, Tracey, Misty and the other Pokémon woke up. They found Ash asleep on top of Charizard.

"Ash," Misty whispered in his ear. "It's time to get up."

"Did Charizard get any better last night?" Tracey asked.

Ash sighed. "Just a little."

Ash climbed off Charizard. The large Pokémon twisted and turned. Then, with a great roar, Charizard stood up and let out a burst of flames.

"It worked, Ash!" Tracey and Misty cried. They all rushed over to hug Charizard.

"*Pika, pika!*" said Pikachu.

"*Scy,*" Scyther hissed. It looked glad that the other Pokémon had got its strength back.

The friends were all congratulating Charizard when they felt a rumble in the earth. Suddenly, a machine that looked like an underground submarine exploded through the ground. The force sent Pikachu flying into the air. Before anyone could stop it, the drill on the front of the machine opened up into two pieces. Pikachu fell right into the middle of the drill and was captured.

Ash couldn't tell what was happening

with all the dust and noise.

"What was that?" Misty shouted.

They didn't have to wait long for an answer. Jessie, James, and Meowth appeared on top of the machine. Team Rocket was at it again!

"Thanks for Pikachu!" Jessie called to Ash.

Ash looked around. Then he noticed Pikachu, trapped in a clear box inside the machine.

"It's the electric-proof box you've all been waiting for," Meowth purred.

"Our years of suffering have finally paid off," added James. "We got you, Pikachu."

"No sense in overstaying our welcome," Jessie sneered.
"Bye-bye!"

Team Rocket jumped back inside the machine. The land submarine quickly tunnelled back underground. Ash ran after them.

"Ash, stop!" Tracey warned. "It's too dangerous."

"I've got to get Pikachu." Ash answered. "I don't care how dangerous it is!"

Charizard flew over and scooped up Ash. "Charizard!" Ash cried thankfully. Charizard headed for the tunnel the machine had made.

"It looks like Charizard really wants to help Ash," Misty remarked.

"I know," agreed Tracey. "But is it strong enough?"

11

A Well-Trained Pokémon

Ash and Charizard followed Team Rocket through the tunnels and back into the daylight. The giant Pokémon roared with anger. Wisps of fire spurted from Charizard's mouth.

"Be careful, Charizard!" Ash warned. "Remember, fire will burn up Pikachu, too!" Ash tried to think of other tactics to use. There was no way he would ever let Pikachu get hurt.

"Charizard," he asked. "Do you think there's any way you can break that machine?"

"*Char!*" the lizard Pokémon roared. Charizard jumped up in the air. Its tremendous feet landed on top of the machine and smashed it open. Pikachu once again flew into the air. Charizard caught the electric-proof box that Pikachu was in and broke the glass with its teeth. Pikachu fell into Ash's arms.

"Pikachu!" Ash cried as he was reunited with his Pokémon. "Thank you, Charizard."

"*Pika, pika,*" Pikachu thanked Charizard.

"You won't get away, Pikachu!" Jessie screamed.

"We've still got our ace in the hole," Meowth howled as he pressed a switch. Sharp, spinning blades appeared on both sides of the machine.

"Look out!" Ash shouted. The blades hit Ash and Pikachu. They both fell off Charizard and were knocked out.

Charizard saw what happened to its trainer. Angry smoke puffed from its snout. Then a colossal ball of fire began spinning inside Charizard's mouth. Streaks of scorching flames shot towards Team Rocket.

"Fire!" James shouted as he ran as fast as he could away from the blaze.

"It's not the season for a heat wave!" cried Jessie.

"Yeeeowwww!" howled Meowth as flames blistered its tail.

The shouting revived Ash and Pikachu. They were amazed. Charizard had never shown fire power like that before. Ash looked at Dexter for an explanation.

"Rage, one of Charizard's most powerful attacks," Dexter

80

explained. "It is a Dragon-type attack that inflicts great damage to the opponent."

As the Rage hit Team Rocket, they were tossed far out into the sea. "Looks like Team Rocket's blasting off again!" they shouted.

Ash and Pikachu flew back to the beach on Charizard's back.

"That was great," Ash said as he hugged Charizard. "You're so cool!"

"Actually, Charizard's so hot," Tracey added with a grin, "he's on fire!"

"You did it, Ash," Misty complimented her friend. "Charizard finally understands how you feel."

"I think this is the beginning of a beautiful friendship," Ash smiled.

"*Char!*" Charizard roared.

A familiar figure walked over and held out his hand to Ash.

"Congratulations, Ash," said Mugsy.

"Mugsy!" said Ash as he shook the other trainer's hand. "Thank you."

"You're welcome," replied Mugsy. "Now, do you think you're ready for a new battle?"

Ash hesitated. He looked at Charizard. Charizard roared its approval.

"Of course!" said Ash. He turned to his Fire Pokémon. "I know you can do this, Charizard. I believe in you."

Mugsy commanded Poliwrath to use Water Gun. Poliwrath blasted water from the middle of its belt. The jet of water headed directly for Charizard.

"Fly, Charizard!" Ash called out.

Charizard quickly flew out of the way.

"Look!" shouted Tracey. "Charizard ducked the attack!"

"That's because it's listening to Ash, now," explained Misty.

Poliwrath followed up with an icy blast. Charizard melted the chilling attack in a fiery blaze.

"This won't end like it did yesterday!" Ash yelled to Mugsy.

"Don't be so sure," Mugsy smirked. "Charizard's a good fighter, but it's not good

enough to beat my Poliwrath. Cold Beam!"
he commanded. Poliwrath spun around
and sent out a shower of ice.

"Fly!" countered Ash. Charizard flew out
of the way.

"Poliwrath, Body Slam!" shouted Mugsy.
Poliwrath got ready to use its muscle power
on Charizard.

Ash thought quickly. "Charizard!" he called. "Seismic Toss!" Charizard got a flying start. It charged at Poliwrath, knocking the Water Pokémon down with its heavy weight. Then Charizard picked up Poliwrath. It flew high into the air, spun around, and sent the Water Pokémon smashing to the ground.

Poliwrath didn't move. It was knocked out.

Ash and Charizard had won the battle!

"We did it, Charizard!" Ash shouted as he hugged the giant creature.

"That was great, Ash," cheered Tracey.

"Great battle, Ash," Mugsy agreed. "Let's do it again some day."

"You're on!" said Ash.

Misty smiled at Ash. "You're on your way to becoming a master trainer," she told him.

"What do you mean, Misty?" Ash asked.

"Now you know the secret to becoming a Pokémon Master isn't power," Misty explained. "It's friendship and teamwork."

"You're right, Misty," Ash agreed. "Charizard would never have listened to me if I didn't understand how it feels."

Ash, Misty and Tracey waved good-bye to Mugsy as he boarded his boat. Ash wanted to get moving, too. He couldn't wait for the next challenge. With Charizard on his side, Ash was one step closer to becoming a Pokémon Master.

About the Author

Tracy West has been writing books for more than ten years. When she's not playing the blue version of the Pokémon game (she started with a Squirtle), she enjoys reading comic books, watching cartoons, and taking long walks in the woods (looking for wild Pokémon). She lives in a small town in New York with her family and pets.